MERMAID SCHOOL

Save Our Seas!

The Mermaid School series

Mermaid School
The Clamshell Show
Ready, Steady, Swim!
All Aboard!
Save our Seas!
The Spooky Shipwreck

Look out for more in the series!
mermaidschoolbooks.co.uk

MERMAID SCHOOL
Save Our Seas!

LUCY COURTENAY
ILLUSTRATED BY SHEENA DEMPSEY

ANDERSEN
PRESS

First published in 2021 by
Andersen Press Limited
20 Vauxhall Bridge Road, London SW1V 2SA, UK
Vijverlaan 48, 3062 HL Rotterdam, Nederland
www.andersenpress.co.uk

2 4 6 8 10 9 7 5 3 1

British Library Cataloguing in Publication Data available.

ISBN 978 1 83913 048 9

Printed and bound in Great Britain
by Clays Ltd, Elcograf S.p.A.

Pearl's House

Galloping Scallop Café

Lord Foam's Atoll Academy

Mermaid Lagoon

Not to scale

School Rock

LADY Barbara

Whale & Hearty

Radio Seawave

Marnie's House

Chapter One

It was warm in the Food Tech Cave at Lady Sealia's Mermaid School, thanks to the hot-water vents steaming and spouting on the cave floor. Marnie Blue carefully swam across the cave with an armful of ingredients and dumped them in her clamshell pot. She pushed a strand of blonde hair out of her eyes and started to stir.

Sweets and Treats was the most popular food tech lesson of the year, because they learned sweetie recipes and tested them out. Everyone's pots bubbled with kelp toffee, air-bubble gum and fizzy whelks. Marnie sniffed happily.

'Marnie!' called Dora Agua. She adjusted her sea-glass goggles and turned up the heat on her hot-water vent. 'Come and watch. This is the cool bit.'

Marnie was surprised to see that Dora's mixture was bright pink. She glanced at the deep green kelp-toffee mixture in her own bubbling pot.

'Are you making fizzy whelks?' she asked.

Dora shook her head. 'I'm inventing something new for my Brinies Inventor badge,' she said with pride. 'I'm going to call it "dolphin poo".'

Marnie wasn't sure she would eat anything called dolphin poo. But she was too nice to say so. 'What's the cool bit I'm supposed to watch?' she asked.

'It's going to turn blue,' said Dora. She stared at the page of seaweed paper in her hand, which was covered in squiggles of squid ink. 'I hope I'm reading my recipe right.'

'What's the deal, moray eel?' said Marnie's best friend Orla Finnegan, swimming across the cave with her long dark hair flowing behind her.

'I'm making dolphin poo,' Dora said.

'What the flippering flippers?' Orla said. 'Dolphin *poo*?'

A red-haired mermaid with steamed-up glasses looked up from her own pot of bubbling green goo. 'Who's making dolphin poo?' she asked with interest.

'I'm not *literally* making dolphin poo, Pearl,' Dora said. 'Because I'm not actually a dolphin. It's a new sweetie recipe I've created for my Brinies Inventor badge.'

Pearl Cockle looked disappointed. She went back to stirring her mixture.

'I don't get this Brinies stuff,' said Orla.

Marnie didn't either, but she was interested to hear about it.

Dora beamed. 'It's krilliant!' she said. 'We do loads of cool stuff, like camping and inventing and building driftwood dens. You should join. Ms Mullet is always looking for new members. Hey, Mabel!' she shouted across the cave.

Mabel Anemone looked up from a mixing bowl. 'Yeah?'

'What are you doing for your Brinies Inventor badge?'

'I've made a cleaning tool which you attach to your tail,' said Mabel. 'It cleans the sea bed in hardly any time. I've called it the Flic-n-Span.'

Dora whistled. 'That sounds orcasome!'

'*I'm* inventing something too,' said Gilly Seaflower. She didn't like it when her friend Mabel got more attention than she did. 'And my invention's JUST as orcasome as Mabel's.'

'What is it then?' said Dora.

Gilly tossed her blonde curls. 'I'm not going to tell YOU. You'll just steal my idea because it's so good.'

'Ignore her, Dora,' said Orla. 'Everyone else does.'

Dora sighed and turned back to her clamshell pot. Her mixture was still pink. 'Why isn't it turning blue?' she said in frustration.

'Maybe you just need to boil it a bit more,' Marnie suggested.

A large octopus with a chunky coral necklace drifted about, tasting everyone's mixtures. It was Miss Tinkle. Monsieur Poisson, the school cook and the food tech teacher, was ill that morning, and Miss Tinkle had enthusiastically volunteered to cover his lesson.

She was enjoying it a little too much, and had already eaten half of Gilly's fizzy whelk mixture and most of Lupita Barracuda's kelp toffee. 'Five starfish minutes, everyone!' she trilled. 'Five more minutes until the end of the lesson!'

'I think something's happening,' said Dora suddenly.

The mixture in her pot was turning a gentle lilac.

'That's blue,' said Dora. She looked hopefully at the others. 'Right?'

'Definitely,' said Marnie.

'Bluer than a blue whale,' agreed Orla.

'What's bluer than a blue whale?' said Pearl, looking up again. Pearl enjoyed conversations about marine life.

'Dora's mixture,' said Marnie.

Pearl adjusted her steamy glasses and peered into Dora's pot. 'I'd say it's more lilac.'

'It's BLUE,' said Marnie firmly.

'DEFINITELY blue,' said Orla.

The tip of a tentacle suddenly swooped into Dora's pot.

'This smells interesting,' said Miss Tinkle. Her eyes shone greedily behind her spectacles. 'Do I smell extract of pearl?'

'Yes, Miss Tinkle,' said Dora. She looked a little anxious at how much of the sweetie mixture was on Miss Tinkle's tentacle. 'I've been experimenting with squid-sucker slime too. I'm entering it for my Brinies Inventor badge.'

'If there's any left,' Orla murmured.

Miss Tinkle licked her tentacle clean. 'Scrumptious,' she said. She scooped up some more and ate it with a happy sucking sound. Then she checked one of the starfish watches on her many wrists. 'Oops. Time to finish your recipes and start clearing up now, mermaids!' And she drifted away.

Marnie, Orla, Pearl and Dora stared at the sad remains of Dora's sweetie mixture.

'That is the smallest dolphin poo I've ever seen,' said Orla.

Marnie patted Dora's shoulder. 'Maybe you only need a tiny bit to win your badge?' she said.

'Maybe,' Dora said glumly.

The mermaids put their pots in the hot-vent dishwashers and wiped the work benches clean.

'I will tell Monsieur Poisson how hard you've all worked today,' said Miss Tinkle, raising her voice over the underwater bell which rang for the end of the lesson. 'Off you go now — oh, *excuse me . . .*'

A small cloud of ink puffed out of Miss Tinkle's behind. It swirled about for a moment, and then disappeared. Miss Tinkle turned red.

'Did Miss Tinkle just parp?' said Pearl.

Orla giggled. Marnie did too.

'Miss Tinkle just parped.' The whisper started spreading. 'Miss Tinkle did a parp . . . did you see? Did you see that cloud of ink?'

'Out you go, mermaids!' said Miss Tinkle, a little shrilly. There was a second little puff of ink. She waved her tentacles hastily.

'Quickly now! Come on!'

'I think she just parped again,' said Pearl.

All the mermaids were giggling now. Some were trying to control their faces. Others, like Orla, weren't trying at all. Marnie was torn between laughing and feeling sorry for her octopus teacher. It must be SUPER embarrassing to parp in front of the class.

'Out!' squealed Miss Tinkle. She rushed out of the cave, leaving another small puff of ink behind. 'Out of my way!'

'I must have added too much squid-sucker slime,' Dora said as the giggling first years all followed their teacher. 'That's why the mixture didn't go blue.'

'Is it just me,' said Pearl, 'or does Miss Tinkle look bigger?'

The octopus was definitely looking rounder. She was floating higher off the rocky floor as well. In fact, she was almost bumping her head on the ceiling of the corridor with her tentacles pressed firmly to her behind. Her face was bright pink.

'She's trying to hold it in,' Marnie said.

'Stop!' Orla leaned against the rocky wall with one hand on her tummy. 'I honestly can't take it. I feel like *my* stomach is going to go pop.'

Miss Tinkle was still rising, getting rounder and rounder. A crowd of mermaids gathered underneath.

'Let it out, Miss Tinkle!' shouted Lupita. 'You know you want to.'

'Miss Tinkle's going to **EXPLODE**!' squealed Gilly.

'What is going on?' Lady Sealia Foam, the head of Mermaid School, swam out of her office into the corridor with her silver dogfish Dilys in her arms. She frowned up at poor Miss Tinkle, who was now stuck to the ceiling.

'Miss Tinkle?' Lady Sealia demanded. 'Why are you on the ceiling?'

'Oh dear,' moaned Miss Tinkle. 'I'm sorry, Lady Sealia, I . . .'

PPPPPPRRRRAAAAAaaaRRRRRRPPP!

Chapter Two

'Begin at the beginning.' Lady Sealia made a steeple out of her fingers and glared across her desk. She looked more frightening than Marnie had ever seen her.

Dora, Pearl, Orla and Marnie floated awkwardly in the middle of Lady Sealia's office. Miss Tinkle sat on the coral stool beside Lady Sealia's desk, sniffing. Curled up on her sea-moss cushion, Dilys was snoring.

'It was an accident,' said Dora.

'It really was, Lady Sealia,' said Marnie.

'Dora forgot the properties of squid-sucker slime,' said Pearl. 'It could happen to anyone. Although probably not me,' she added, thoughtfully.

'Orla?' said Lady Sealia in her chilliest voice. 'Do you have anything to add?'

Orla shook her head. Marnie realised her best friend had stuffed a seaweed hankie into her mouth to stop herself from laughing out loud.

'Of course it wasn't an accident!' Miss Tinkle spluttered. She pointed a tentacle at Marnie. 'Remember who Marnie Blue is related to, Lady Sealia! This is just the sort of prank *Christabel Blue* enjoyed when she was at the school!'

Marnie gaped at her octopus teacher. It was unfortunately true that her aunt Christabel had been extremely naughty before becoming the most famous singer and radio presenter in Mermaid Lagoon. Marnie loved her aunt, but that didn't mean she was the same. She tried SO HARD to be good. Miss Tinkle was being very unfair.

'I'm not like my aunt, Miss Tinkle,' she said. 'You know I'm not!'

Miss Tinkle narrowed her eyes. 'Everyone says that BLOOD IS THICKER THAN SEAWATER.'

'Detention, Marnie Blue,' said Lady Sealia.

'That's completely unfair,' said Pearl in indignation.

'It wasn't even her sweetie mixture,' protested Dora. 'It was mine.'

Orla pulled the seaweed hankie out of her mouth. 'Miss Tinkle shouldn't have eaten so much of it,' she said. 'None of this is Marnie's fault. And if you can't see that, you're the worst headteacher in the whole lagoon!'

Marnie squeaked and covered her mouth. No one ever spoke to Lady Sealia like that.

'See what I have to deal with, Lady Sealia,' moaned Miss Tinkle.

'Detention,' Lady Sealia repeated, louder. 'For **ALL** of you! There is an unusual amount of plastic rubbish on our fishball pitch today. You can all go out there and clean it up.' She picked up Dilys, who yawned and wriggled. 'Come, Dilys. I am taking you for swimmies until I have calmed down. If that fishball pitch isn't clean when I get back, I will have something to say about it.'

And she swam out of the office with Dilys behind her.

'Thanks for sticking up for me, guys,' said Marnie.

Orla put her arm around Marnie's shoulders. 'Lady Sealia and Miss Tinkle were out of order, blaming you like that.'

'Mates back each other up,' said Dora.

'Through thick and fin,' said Pearl.

Marnie felt a rush of gratitude. 'You're all the best,' she said.

Litter lay scattered across the fishball pitch in front of them. There were plastic bottles and tangled plastic bags, plastic straws and bottle lids. Everything was covered with one word: *McMeaty's.*

'Where has all this stuff come from?' asked Dora.

'Humans, of course,' said Orla in disgust.

Marnie thought about her aunt Christabel's old boyfriend, Arthur. He was human. He wouldn't drop junk like this in Mermaid Lagoon, would he? Humans were a mystery, she thought.

'I think we should split up,' she said. 'It'll be quicker that way.'

Orla handed out the school's driftwood brooms and

seaweed nets for carrying the trash away. Then they swam slowly to the four corners of the fishball pitch.

Sweeping was tricky. If Marnie swept too hard, all the junk whooshed up high in the water and swirled around her head before landing on the sea bed again. And if she swept too softly, the junk didn't move at all. She chased the same bottle around the same patch of the fishball pitch for ages before putting the broom down and catching the bottle in her hands. It felt hard and strange. Not mermaidy at ALL. Panting a little, she put it into her seaweed net.

Orla had dumped her driftwood broom and was trying to use her tail to flap the junk into her seaweed net. It wasn't working. Pearl had put her broom down and was studying a family of starfish that had set up home on one of the fishball goalposts. Dora had built a broom extension, adding four spiny sea urchins to the ends of the driftwood bristles.

'What are you doing with those sea urchins?' Marnie asked.

'I've got a new invention for my Brinies Inventor badge,' said Dora with enthusiasm. 'I'm using the sea urchins to spike up the rubbish. It's working really well.'

She pushed the broom at a heap of junk. Several bottle tops got stuck on the sea urchins' spines.

'I'm going to call it the Spike-u-Like,' said Dora proudly.

Marnie thought the sea urchins looked a bit cross. 'I don't think they're enjoying it much,' she said.

'They're fine,' said Dora. 'I'll just . . . oh . . .'

The two biggest sea urchins wriggled off the broom and started fighting. One of the sea urchins shot into

Dora's face and spiked her nose. All the bottle tops fell off and swirled around in a haze of blue and green and red.

'Ow!' said Dora.

A sudden current swept across the sea bed. It picked up all the plastic Dora had been collecting and pushed it to the far side of the pitch. It also wrenched Marnie's seaweed net out of her hands and showered the contents all over the ground again.

'There's more plastic than when we started,' groaned Orla. 'It's like all the bottles are having baby bottles or something.'

Marnie wondered how long it would be before Lady Sealia returned, and what would happen if they hadn't cleaned up the pitch.

'Come on,' she said wearily. 'Most of it went that way.'

Orla and Dora followed Marnie to the furthest corner of the fishball pitch. Pearl beat her tail and zoomed hastily after them, showering them with starfish facts as they swam. 'Did you know that a starfish doesn't have a brain? Did you know a starfish isn't actually a fish at all? Did you know—'

'What's that?' said Marnie suddenly.

There was something on the edge of the fishball pitch. Something large, and grey, and very, very still. A long grey nose poked out of a tangle of plastic netting. A small black eye fluttered for a moment.

It was a dolphin.

Chapter
Three

For a moment, the mermaids were too shocked to say anything. They saw dolphins around, of course, but they were wild creatures that never came too close to the mermaids.

The dolphin twitched. Her fins were hopelessly tangled in the netting, and her beak was wedged in one of the netting holes.

'She's stuck,' said Dora.

'Anyone can see that,' said Orla.

The dolphin looked so still and sad, as if she had given up. Marnie felt a terrible lump in her throat.

'We have to help her, Marnie!' Pearl said. 'Dolphins don't breathe water like us. They need air! If she doesn't get to the surface, she's going to DROWN.'

'My parents say you should never approach a wild animal,' said Dora. Her parents were marine vets, with a cool selection of 'I've been as good as goldfish' stickers which they gave to their patients. 'But if we don't approach this one, I think she might die.'

Marnie swam cautiously over to the dolphin. She tugged at the netting. She didn't move at all.

'Can we cut her free?' said Orla.

Marnie caught the shadow of something out of the corner of her eye. For one horrible moment she thought it was a shark. Then she saw the long, serrated blade jutting out of the creature's nose, and realised her mistake.

'A swordfish,' said Orla, following Marnie's gaze.

'*Sailfish*,' Pearl corrected. 'Swordfish have smooth blades. Sailfish have serrated blades.'

Marnie stared at the sailfish.

'Are you thinking what I'm thinking?' said Orla.

'If you're thinking about catching that sailfish and using its blade to cut the dolphin free,' said Marnie, 'then I totally AM thinking what you're thinking.'

'Its blade looks super sharp,' said Dora anxiously.

'That's the point,' said Pearl.

Dora sat beside the trapped dolphin and made soothing noises as Pearl, Orla and Marnie swam towards the sailfish.

'After three,' said Pearl. 'One . . . two . . . THREE!'

Marnie, Orla and Pearl jumped on to the sailfish. It thrashed about indignantly in their arms.

'We just need to borrow you for a second,' said Pearl. 'We won't hurt you.'

Pearl guided the wriggling sailfish towards the dolphin, almost cutting herself on its flashing blade. Marnie and Orla pushed from behind. Together, they managed to hook the blade through the net. Then they pulled.

The net split. Just a little. The dolphin feebly lifted her head as the mermaids pulled the sailfish's blade through the net again. More of the netting fell away. The dolphin flicked her tail. The light was back in her eyes.

'One . . . more . . . go . . .' panted Pearl.

The sailfish suddenly pulled itself free. Before they could grab it again, it swam away, disappearing into the distance faster than Marnie could have ever imagined. The mermaids stayed where they were, tugging desperately at the net.

Marnie felt a blow on her side as the dolphin thrashed her tail. She gazed up towards the surface of the lagoon. It was a long way up. The dolphin was tired. The more she struggled, the more air she was using.

'We have to take her to the surface,' she told the others.

They lifted the dolphin together. More netting came away from under her belly. She really was fighting now. The mermaids swam up as hard as they could, carrying the dolphin towards the light. *Nearly there*, thought Marnie. Her arms were aching. *Nearly there . . .*

With a burst of light and air, they broke the surface. Marnie felt the wind in her hair as the dolphin took a joyful breath through her blowhole. Orla and Dora whooped.

'We did it!' shouted Pearl, whacking the surface of the water with her hand.

Marnie helped the others to unpick what was left of the netting. The dolphin was getting livelier, chittering and whistling away.

'We're the bream team!' said Orla, high-fiving Marnie.

'Thank you,' said a clicking, whistling voice.

Marnie, Pearl, Orla and Dora all jumped. The dolphin had spoken! Marnie had heard about the magic of dolphins, and how they spoke in very special circumstances. She never thought she'd hear one herself.

'Wow,' she stammered. She suddenly felt shy. 'Hi!'

The dolphin's black eyes were bright and serious. 'I would have died without your help,' she said.

'You're totally welcome,' said Orla, recovering.

Pearl gazed at the dolphin in delight.

'Orcasome,' Dora whispered.

'Let me know if you ever need help,' said the dolphin. 'I owe you my life. Just call my name, and I'll come.'

'Wow!' said Marnie again. 'We will!'

'What IS your name?' Pearl asked, in a practical sort of way.

27

The dolphin whistled and clicked a complicated sequence of notes. *Peep peep CLICK CLICK-CLICK click click PEEEEP.* 'Call my name,' she said again, 'and I will come.'

The dolphin flipped her tail and arced out of the

water. Then, with a great splash, she disappeared beneath the surface and was gone.

'We're never going to remember that name,' said Pearl.

'Think of it as a rhythm, Pearl,' suggested Orla.

'Like . . . Gil-ly SEA-FLO-WER is-a-TWIT.'

Marnie stared after the dolphin. 'Did that really just happen?' she asked.

'My parents won't believe me when I tell them!' Dora squealed.

The four mermaids did a little happy dance, holding hands and giggling. They'd spoken to a dolphin. How crayfish crazy was that?

The bottom of the sea bed was a long way down, but it felt like no distance at all. Marnie raced her friends, laughing and spinning in the water. Orla and Dora started singing 'In It to Fin It', the hit song that was all over Radio SeaWave. Marnie joined in.

'I think this is the best day of my life,' said Pearl breathlessly.

From up here, Marnie could see a strange, multi-coloured carpet spread far below. There were blues, and reds, and greens, and pinks, and all kinds of strange colours and shapes. Marnie frowned.

'What's that stuff all around School Rock?' said Orla.

They swam closer. The colours and shapes slowly began to turn into objects. Bottles, and straws, and boxes, and oddly shaped things. Everything was

covered with the same word as before: *McMeaty's*. It lay everywhere, drifting into heaps and swirling about.

The mermaids slowed to a stop and hung in the water above the brightly coloured carpet of junk.

'Plastic,' said Marnie in dismay. 'It's more plastic!'

Chapter Four

From up here, the mermaids could see how far the plastic stretched. It rippled around the bottom of School Rock like a tatty, brightly coloured tutu.

'And I thought the litter on the fishball pitch was bad,' said Orla.

'Think of all the dolphins who could get caught in THAT!' said Pearl.

And not just dolphins, thought Marnie. Fish big and small, and eels, and crabs, and whales, and sharks. Everyone who lived in Mermaid Lagoon was going to be affected.

'We have to clean it up,' Marnie said. 'Right away! Every moment that goes by, an animal's life is in danger!'

The others all started talking over each other.

'There's too much of it!' said Pearl.

'Can't we just tell the teachers?' said Dora.

'We can't do it by ourselves,' said Orla.

'Exactly, Orla,' Marnie said. 'We can't do it by ourselves. We have to organise everyone to help. I need to talk to my aunt.'

'Could your aunt put it out on Radio SeaWave?' Pearl asked.

'That's what I'm going to ask,' said Marnie. 'If Christabel talks about it on her *Big Blue Show,* then **EVERYONE** will come and help after school tomorrow.'

'It's the Ultra Fishball League Final after school tomorrow,' Dora pointed out. 'Everyone's going to be watching it on the new Sea-V at the Galloping Scallop.'

Pearl's dad had recently hung a Sea-V screen on the Galloping Scallop café wall to show the Ultra Fishball Final. A huge conch-shell receiver sat on the roof of the café. Three handles set into the café wall had to be pumped up and down to keep the pictures coming.

Marnie frowned at the mention of the Fishball Final. She wasn't going to float about and watch her beautiful lagoon fill up with yucky plastic. She felt sure that everyone else would feel the same. 'Mermaid Lagoon is more important than fishball,' she said. 'Let's finish clearing up the school fishball pitch, and then head over to Radio SeaWave. Come on!'

At sea-bed level, it was difficult to understand how big the problem was. But Marnie couldn't forget the mess all around School Rock.

Christabel was recording in the booth at Radio SeaWave as Marnie and the others arrived. Flip and Sam, the producer and sound engineer of the show, looked up from their mixing desks as the four mermaids swam in.

'. . . time for everyone's favourite part of the show, Dance 'n' Dazzle!' Christabel was saying, her shell headphones over her ears and her blonde hair piled on the top of her head. 'Dave Driftwood from Saline Avenue says, "Can you play 'Whelkcome One and All' for my wife Kelpia? Kelpia helped me pickle lots of sea-urchin eggs last night." Well, Dave, you know what they say

about dancing on pickled sea-urchin eggs. You might end up with more of a "SMELLcome One and All", if you know what I mean. But here it is. Get your dancing tails on!'

'Whelkcome One and All' started blasting through the speakers. It was an oldies tune, in Marnie's opinion. But Christabel had a wide fanbase in Mermaid Lagoon, with listeners from eight to eighty, so you never knew what she would play next.

'What's up, Marnie?' said Sam.

'We have a problem,' said Marnie. She explained about all the plastic swishing around the bottom of School Rock. 'Can Christabel make an announcement at the end of the show? Tell everyone to meet us at School Rock tomorrow afternoon for the clean-up?'

Sam scratched his beard. 'The Ultra Fishball League Final's on tomorrow afternoon,' he said. 'Everyone will be watching that.'

'That's not important, though,' Marnie said. 'Not like our lagoon.'

'If you say so,' Sam said doubtfully.

He put on his headphones again to pass the message to Christabel. Marnie swam over to join the others. They were all making a fuss over Christabel's pet goldfish, Garbo, who was curled up in her bowl in the corner of the studio.

'Is Christabel going to put out the message?' Pearl asked.

Marnie nodded. 'And then we'll have loads of volunteers tomorrow and we'll clean everything up in no time at all,' she said confidently.

A squeal on the bladder-wrack bagpipes brought 'Whelkome One and All' to a bouncing stop.

'What a smashing tune that is,' said Christabel cheerfully. She waved out of the booth window at Marnie and her friends. 'Now, I have an important announcement to make, so pull that seaweed out of your

ears and listen up. There's going to be a litter-picking posse out tomorrow at half past the afternoon starfish, clearing a load of plastic that's washed up around School Rock. Come and do your bit for our environment, folks. *Sea* you there!'

'Was that your idea, Orla?' asked Sheela Finnegan, Orla's sister. Sheela worked at Radio SeaWave too, helping Christabel on her shows and keeping everything clean and tidy in the studio. 'The litter-picking thing?'

'It was Marnie's,' said Orla.

'We're saving the lagoon,' Marnie said. 'You won't believe how much plastic is out there. You'll be there tomorrow afternoon, right?'

'I'm watching the Ultra Fishball League Final with my mates at the Galloping Scallop tomorrow,' Sheela said. 'You guys should come along. It's going to be a really tight match. The Flying Flounders are the champions of course, they'll defend their title for sure.'

Flip looked up from the mixing desk. 'I think you mean the Raving Rays, Sheela. Everyone knows the *Floundering* Flounders don't have a hope.'

Sheela rolled her eyes. 'The Rays are wetter than

a baby haddock's nappy, Flip,' she said. 'And you know it.'

'But you **WILL** be at the clean-up, won't you?' Marnie said, a little anxiously. 'This is the lagoon we're talking about. It's such a mess! Think about the wildlife!'

'I guess,' said Sheela. 'If I can. Like, after the Ultra Fishball League Final or something.' And she drifted away with her sea sponge to clean the algae off the Christabel Blue posters on the rocky walls of the studio.

All of a sudden, Marnie wasn't so certain about her plan.

'I'm sure a few volunteers will come,' said Orla. 'Not everyone's into Ultra Fishball.'

'But we don't need a few,' said Marnie, feeling worried. 'We need LOADS.'

What were they going to do if nobody turned up?

Chapter
Five

'Right,' said Marnie. She shouldered her placard. 'After me. ONE, TWO, THREE, FOUR, NO McMEATY'S ANY MORE!'

No one had turned up that afternoon to help clear the plastic. No one at all. Marnie couldn't believe it. Didn't anyone understand how important this was? Now she had a new plan, involving placards at the Galloping Scallop café, where everyone was watching the Ultra Fishball League Final.

Most of the customers had their backs to the window so they could watch the Sea-V. A few glanced out of the window at the placards before glancing away again.

'ONE, TWO, THREE, FOUR,' chanted Orla. 'NO McMEATY'S ANY MORE!'

'ONE, TWO, THREE, FOUR,' said Dora. 'Hey, check out the fishball score.'

'That's not the words,' said Pearl. Her pet angelfish, Sparkle, swam through Pearl's hair, and nibbled at the gold lettering which spelled out NO FISH = NO FUN on Pearl's placard.

Dora blushed. 'Sorry,' she said. 'I just saw the score through the window. The Raving Rays are *smashing* the Flying Flounders seven-three!'

Dora's own placard said BRINIES UNITE! IT'S TIME TO FIGHT! (the plastic).

'ONE, TWO, THREE, FOUR,' shouted Marnie in determination.

Everyone in the café roared. The score was now eight-three.

Pearl's dad put his head round the door. 'Are you OK out here, love?' he asked Pearl, wiping his hands on his apron. 'It's two-for-one on my salted sea-urchin cookies today. Why don't you have a break and pop in for a bit?'

'Ooh!' said Dora, lowering her placard.

'Dora!' said Marnie. 'This is IMPORTANT.'

Sheepishly, Dora lifted her placard up again.

'Tell you what,' said Pearl's dad. 'I'll bring out a few cookies for you.'

'Thanks, Mr Cockle,' said Marnie. She lifted her **STAY IN TUNE, SAVE OUR LAGOON!** placard higher. '**ONE, TWO, THREE, FOUR, NO McMEATY'S ANY MORE! ONE, TWO, THREE, FOUR . . .**'

'This is all a massive bore,' said Orla.

'Those aren't the words either,' said Pearl.

'It's hopeless,' said Orla. She dropped her placard face down on the sea bed. 'Nobody cares.'

Marnie's eyes filled with tears. 'But everything is ruined with all this horrible McMeaty's stuff everywhere. What if another dolphin gets tangled up? Or our pets are injured?'

Pearl looked worried. She scooped up Sparkle for a cuddle. Marnie felt flatter than a flatfish. She had no idea how to fix the situation. It was a horrible feeling.

There was another roar.

'**ONE, TWO, THREE, FOUR!**' someone shouted from inside the café. 'Go the Flounders, eight-four!'

On Friday morning, there was more plastic than ever. It blew around the coral and lay in heaps around the sea bed. Bottles drifted around like strange fish. Transparent rings of plastic bobbed along like silent jellyfish.

'This is rubbish,' said Orla furiously, swimming beside Marnie on their way to school. 'Literally RUBBISH.'

Marnie hitched her pearl backpack over her shoulder and stared unhappily at the mess. The lagoon looked scruffy and awful.

'What is all this horrible McMeaty's stuff?' said Gilly, swimming up with Lupita.

'And why is it all here?' said Lupita. She untangled a plastic straw from her hair and stuffed it into her backpack.

Gilly pushed a floating plastic McMeaty's tub out of her way. 'I can't *bear* mess,' she said fussily. 'A nice environment is SO important to me.'

'Then you should have come to yesterday's clean-up,' said Orla.

Gilly flushed. 'I was busy.'

Orla laughed. 'Busy trying to impress the fishball-watching merboys at the Galloping Scallop yesterday. I saw you through the window.'

'Has anyone seen Pearl?' Marnie asked.

Pearl usually joined them on their way into school.

The others shook their heads.

'At least we have PE first thing to cheer us up,' said Lupita, who loved sport.

'Ha ha,' said Orla, who didn't.

When they got to school, a row of teachers were outside the Assembly Cave, trying to keep the litter outside the school. Marnie's classmates had gathered in a whispering group, waiting until they could all go inside.

'WAFT it,' Lady Sealia said, swimming up and down in front of the teachers. She waved her tail at a bottle that was trying to sneak into the cave. The bottle swooshed away. Dilys zoomed after it, then swam back to Lady Sealia with the bottle in her mouth. 'NO, Dilys. NAUGHTY, Dilys.'

Len the lionfish librarian was having the most success, thanks to all his fins. Miss Tinkle was punching the plastic with some force, sending bottles and boxes and junk shooting off in all directions. Ms Mullet the crab deputy head and Mr Scampi the lobster oceanography teacher's claws weren't much use, but they were doing their best. Miss Haddock — the

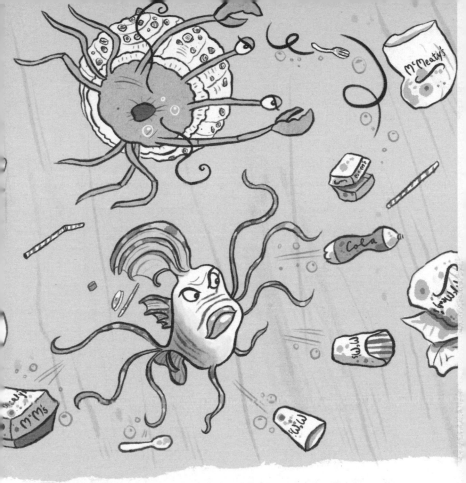

PE teacher — kept talking to the plastic as if it could hear her: 'GO AWAY PLEASE. PLEASE GET AWAY FROM ME.' Marnie could see that a few bottles had still sneaked into the Assembly Cave, despite the teachers' best efforts.

'Move inside, mermaids,' Miss Tinkle said breathlessly. WHACK. WALLOP. 'In you go!'

'We could miss registration and go straight to PE,' said Lupita hopefully.

'We're not having PE, Lupita dear,' said Miss Haddock. Her catfish Cecil happily chased straws around Miss Haddock's tail. **'GET AWAY FROM ME PLEASE.** Not you, Mabel. **PLEASE LEAVE AND DON'T COME BACK.** Not you, Orla.'

'The fishball pitch is covered in plastic,' panted Miss Tinkle. 'Today we shall all be having exam practice in the Sports Cave instead. Lady Sealia, have you ever considered installing doors to the Assembly Cave?'

'NO PE?' said Lupita in horror. 'Exam practice instead?'

Lupita hadn't come to the clean-up on Saturday either. Marnie decided not to point this out.

'PLEASE GET OUT OF MY SIGHT. Not you, Lupita,' said Miss Haddock. Cecil hurtled past Lupita's nose with his whiskers bristling.

Lady Sealia noticed Marnie. 'Marnie Blue!' she barked. 'I told you and your friends to clean up this mess two days ago!'

Marnie felt hot and cold all at once. 'We tried, Lady Sealia,' she stammered, 'but there was too much of it! And now there's more! It's not our fault, honestly!'

52

Pearl swam up with Dora, holding Sparkle under one arm. 'Have I missed registration?' she said. 'I had to take Sparkle to see Dora's dad.'

'Sparkle cut her fins on a broken McMeaty's bottle,' Dora explained. 'We need to fix this problem before more pets get hurt.'

To Marnie's relief, Lady Sealia had turned away. She stared at the tiny bandages on Sparkle's fins. She wanted to whack her tail against the sea bed, and shout, and yell. None of this was Sparkle's fault, or the trapped dolphin's fault, or the fault of anyone who lived on the sea bed.

'We **HAVE** to find out where the plastic is coming from,' she said angrily. 'And then we **HAVE** to make it stop.'

Mabel scratched her ear. 'Why don't we ask Ms Mullet about it at Brinies tonight?'

'Krilliant idea!' said Dora.

'Where's the meeting, Dora?' said Marnie. 'Can I come?'

Dora brightened. 'Of course! We usually meet by the stables.'

'You'll come too, won't you, Orla?' said Marnie. 'And you, Pearl?'

Orla nodded a little reluctantly. She wasn't much of a joiner. Pearl nodded too, and stroked Sparkle. Marnie felt a tiny bit better. With the help of Ms Mullet and the Brinies, perhaps they would be able to solve the problem after all.

'Tonight then,' said Dora. 'Straight after school. And you can see for yourself how much fun Brinies is.'

'Done!' said Marnie.

Chapter
Six

'All together now, Brinies!' Ms Mullet said.

The crab deputy head clacked her claws at the little group of mermaids gathered in front of the seahorse stables. She had a peculiar hat on, with a frond of seaweed sticking out of it. All the Brinies wore green sea-silk scarves, including Dora, Mabel and Gilly. A couple of the school seahorses put their heads over their oyster-shell doors to see what the noise was about.

'I promise I will do my best, for friend, for family, for guest. Brinie law and Brinie fun, I'll do it all, till all is done,' Dora, Mabel and Gilly recited, while Marnie, Orla and Pearl listened.

'We're going to sing a song now,' Dora told Marnie. 'Just follow us.'

All the mermaids started dancing and singing in little groups of six.

'Come let us make a Brinie ring,' sang Dora.

'A Brinie ring, a Brinie ring . . .' With a bit of giggling and tail-bumping, Marnie, Orla and Pearl joined hands with Dora, Mabel and Gilly. *'Come let us make a Brinie ring, we hear our Brown Bass calling.'*

Marnie wondered what a Brown Bass was.

'Widdle!' said Ms Mullet, a little surprisingly.

'Widdle!' chorused the Brinies.

'Widdle piddle!'

'Widdle piddle!'

'Widdle widdle **WEE** piddle!'

'Widdle, widdle, **WEE** *piddle!'*

'Ping, pang, po,' finished Ms Mullet.

'Ping, pang, po,' chorused the rest of the Brinies. There was a burst of clapping.

'What did that even mean?' asked Orla.

'It's just something we say,' Dora said.

'Can I get a green scarf?' said Orla.

'As **IF**,' said Gilly.

'You have to take the pledge,' Mabel explained.

Ms Mullet adjusted her hat. 'Brinies!' she said. 'Mabel Anemone and Dora Agua have asked this troop to look into the plastic problem that we are having in the lagoon. All in favour, say "fish".'

'Fish!' said the Brinies.

'I have already had a discussion with Lord Foam and his Sea Trouts,' Ms Mullet said. 'We have agreed to join forces to answer the question that is on everyone's lips.'

'Is the question about getting a green scarf?' said Orla.

'The question is this,' said Ms Mullet. 'Where is this plastic coming from? What is McMeaty's? And how can we make it stop?'

'That's three questions,' said Pearl.

'Who are the Sea Trouts?' Marnie asked.

'Don't you know *anything*?' said Gilly. She stroked her green scarf. 'The Sea Trouts come from Atoll Academy.'

'Brown Bass is taking this very seriously,' Dora said.

'Do you mean Ms Mullet?' asked Pearl.

'Brown Bass is Ms Mullet's Brinies title,' explained Mabel. 'Lord Foam is Chief Sea Trout for the merboys.'

'The Sea Trouts will be joining us shortly,' said Ms Mullet. 'While we wait, we have two Inventor badges to award! Please welcome Mabel Anemone with her interesting cleaning concept, Flic-n-Span.'

There was more clapping. Mabel swam up, grinning and waving her Flic-n-Span invention at her friends.

Ms Mullet pinned Mabel's badge on to her green scarf. 'We also have Gilly Seaflower and her, ah, Cleany Tail!' she said.

Gilly swam on to the stage, waving even harder than Mabel.

'Per-lease,' Orla snorted. 'A Cleany Tail? It's identical to Mabel's Flic-n-Span, only with a worse name.'

The space in front of the seahorse stables was suddenly full of merboys, chattering and laughing and pushing each other around. Lord Foam bobbed around in the middle, adjusting the long sea-moss sash around his waist.

'Good evening, Brown Bass,' said Chief Foam. 'Sorry we're late. Tuna traffic.'

'Welcome, Chief Sea Trout,' said Ms Mullet.

Lord Foam turned to his troop. 'Sea Trouts, present fins!'

The merboys floated to attention. Marnie waved at her friend Eddy and his mate Algie.

They waved back before Lord Foam glared at them and they stopped.

'They've got scarves too,' said Orla, staring at the Sea Trouts' sea-moss sashes.

'The plastic is coming into the lagoon from the south,' Lord Foam told the assembled Brinies and Sea Trouts. 'I propose that we swim in that direction this evening, track the source and clean up as much as we can.'

'All those in favour, say "fish",' said Ms Mullet.

'FISH!' Marnie shouted with everyone else.

'Swim in groups of three or more,' instructed Ms Mullet. 'And watch out for the usual hazards. Reef sharks, stingrays, slow-moving tuna.'

'Aye aye, Brown Bass!' cried the Brinies.

'Sea Trouts, formation swim!' said Lord Foam.

'Aye aye, Chief Sea Trout!' cried the Sea Trouts.

Everyone was given a seaweed net to tuck into their backpacks, ready for the clean-up.

'This is a good chance to test my Flic-n-Span,' said Mabel.

'I'm going to clean up TWICE as much as anyone else with my Cleany Tail because it's so amazing,' Gilly added.

It was all pretty exciting, Marnie thought, as they flocked away from School Rock. The Brinies swam together in little huddles, squealing every time a large fish came too close. The Sea Trouts swam in smart lines, like the guards at Queen Maretta's palace, with their sashes floating behind them. Someone behind Marnie started singing a Brinies song. Everyone joined in. It was a cheery tune, and Marnie soon got the gist of it.

'Brinies, Brinies, one two three!
Brinies, Brinies, you and me!
All fins together! All fins together!
We're Brinies all together!'

'SWIM, two, three, four,' shouted Lord Foam at his Sea Trout troops. 'SWIM, two, three, four!' And the song and the rhythm fitted together pretty well.

'Ooh,' said Pearl suddenly, after they had been swimming and singing for almost a full starfish hour.

She pointed at a group of long, thin brown fish clustered around a rock on the sea bed. 'Clingfish! Clingfish can pull limpets off rocks. *Schlurp!* Just like that.'

Dora looked interested. 'How?'

'They have really powerful suckers on their bellies to hold them on the rock while they're eating the limpets,' Pearl said. *'Schlurp!'* she added, again.

The sea bed was getting shallow. Drifts of McMeaty's plastic lay in heaps on the smooth sand. Everyone put their heads above the surface a little nervously. They were always told never to get too close to the shore — and there it was, the shore, all glittering with sand and . . .

'I believe we have found the source of the problem, Chief Sea Trout,' said Ms Mullet.

'Indeed we have, Brown Bass,' said Lord Foam.

Marnie stared at the plastic-strewn beach in front of them. She saw bottles and straws, and boxes and tangles of plastic rings. There were a couple of goal posts set into the sand, with half a net flapping about in the breeze. Marnie wondered if the missing part of the net was the part which had trapped the dolphin.

She could hear something drifting on the air. A *thump-thump-thump* that made her tail twitch. It was music.

'I like that tune,' said Orla. Her tail was twitching too.

'I believe humans call it a *music festival*,' said Lord Foam.

'Cool,' said Eddy, staring at the shore.

Gilly was already scooting around the sea bed whisking at the plastic with her Cleany Tail. 'I'm collecting LOADS,' she shouted as she whisked past.

Marnie, Pearl and Orla filled their nets alongside Dora, Eddy and Algie. Mabel's Flic-n-Span fell off and had to be fixed on again. Gilly grew redder and redder in the face as she chased the same bottle round and round with her Cleany Tail. Several Sea Trouts were messing around, catching each other with the seaweed nets instead of filling them with litter.

'What are we going to do with our nets, Brown Bass?' asked Dora when every net was full.

'Leave them neatly among the rocks over there,' said Ms Mullet, pointing at the shore. 'It's time to head home and make our report to Lady Sealia.'

Marnie frowned.

'But we haven't solved the problem, Ms Mullet,' she said. 'We've just tidied up a bit. We still don't know where the plastic is COMING from.'

'There is human clothing on that beach, Marnie,' Ms Mullet said. 'Which means that humans will be swimming nearby. I can't put you in that kind of danger. Nets on the rocks, please!'

Everyone piled their nets among the rocks for the humans to find and take away.

'Sea Trouts, form a line!' cried Lord Foam.

'Brinies, let's go!' called Ms Mullet.

Marnie dug her tail into the sand. 'I'm not leaving until I know what McMeaty's is and how we can stop it from littering our lagoon,' she said. 'And I'm going ashore to find out.'

Dora, Mabel and Gilly all gasped.

'I'm going ashore with Marnie,' said Orla. Her tail was still twitching in time to the *thump-thump-thump* of the music.

'Me too,' squeaked Pearl. Sparkle popped out of the top of her jumper, and then popped down again.

'But we're *Brinies*,' Gilly said, still red in the face from her Cleany Tail efforts. She put her hand on her green sea-silk scarf. 'We made a pledge about Brinie law and that means doing what Brown Bass says.'

'But WE don't have scarves,' Orla pointed out, a little triumphantly. 'And WE didn't make the pledge. So WE don't have to do what Brown Bass says.'

'I guess you can do what you like, Marnie,' Dora said, exchanging troubled looks with Mabel. 'See you later.'

Gilly tossed her curls. 'If the humans don't catch and eat you first!'

Chapter
Seven

Humans wore the *weirdest* things. Marnie's top was made of something soft and white, with a sparkly heart shape in the middle that scratched and tickled her arms. As for the itchy blue wrapping around her legs . . . well. Legs were weird, whatever you wrapped them in.

Orla was wearing a bright orange, bag-like dress. Pearl had found a thick, soft top lying on the beach, with long sleeves and a baggy hem. It hung down past the knobbly bits in the middle of Pearl's pale legs that Marnie thought were called *knees*. Sparkle watched a little anxiously from the water, tied to a rock close to the shore so that she wouldn't get lost.

Now what? Orla mouthed at Marnie.

For mermaids, climbing ashore and growing legs came with one big drawback. They lost their voices. It was freaky, especially as Marnie and her friends spent so much of their time chatting and laughing and singing underwater. But they had agreed that this was an emergency, and was worth the sacrifice. Orla also wanted to check out the music festival, because it sounded amazing.

They **LOOKED** like humans with legs and clothes and everything, thought Marnie. So what was the harm? They would just take a peek, and find out what McMeaty's was, and stop the plastic junk from getting into the lagoon any more, and then return to the water and swim home. She was a little hazy on the details, if she was honest.

I don't like this, Pearl mouthed. She looked a bit trembly. Unlike Marnie and Orla, she had never been ashore before.

It's going to be **FINE**, Marnie mouthed back.

There was a *floof* sound as Orla fell over in the sand. Marnie fell over too. Pearl fell on top of them both. Legs were hard. When they were upright again, they started towards the music in a wobbly line. Marnie began dancing absent-mindedly, and fell over for a second time.

A hand reached down to help her up. It was Eddy, the Atoll Academy merboy.

What are you doing here, Eddy? Orla mouthed.

70

And what are you wearing?

Eddy looked down at his sparkly dress. He waved at the beach. *Found it over there.* He then did a strange shimmy, which Marnie supposed was meant to be human dancing, and cupped his ear. Marnie guessed he wanted to listen to the music, like Orla. Algie popped up behind Eddy, danced and cupped his ear too. He was wearing a dress as well.

The three mermaids and two merboys moved down the path towards the music. It was louder now, with a thrilling rhythm that made Marnie want to sing — only, of course, she couldn't. *I'm here for the plastic,* she reminded herself. *That's all.*

Finally, they reached a wide space with a stage.

Marnie stared.

Humans of every size and shape and colour danced around the space to the music pouring from the stage. They wore hats, and long flowing gowns, and tight-fitting leg things, and no leg things at all. Their hair was long, short, curly, pink, spiky. Their feet were covered in brightly coloured things Marnie couldn't even name. Flags fluttered overhead, and multicoloured lights flashed. Over everything, the music thumped and rang and shook.

Orla's eyes glowed. She grabbed Eddy's hand and towed him into the crowd to dance. Pearl and Algie hovered nervously on the edge with Marnie.

I don't want to leave Sparkle too long, Pearl mouthed at Marnie, shaking her head and pointing at the sea. She hitched up her baggy top and pulled an anxious face.

Marnie's eye was caught by something flashing near the stage. A sign.

McMEATY'S FESTIVAL TAKEAWAY FOOD!

Marnie walked towards the McMeaty's sign. She stared at the familiar bottles, cups, boxes and straws. This was it! This was the start of the whole problem, **RIGHT HERE!**

'What can I get you, love?' said a lady in a McMeaty's apron.

Marnie shook her head and backed away. Her foot caught on an uneven bit of ground, and she toppled backwards. Just in time, she grabbed hold of someone's sleeve.

'Steady!' said a voice.

Marnie looked up.

Straight into the face of Christabel's human ex-boyfriend, Arthur Bagshot.

She knew it was Arthur right away. She'd seen his eyes through his funny breathing mask the day he'd shown up at the Clamshell Show. They were bright blue and completely unmistakable.

'You look very familiar,' said Arthur, frowning.

Struggling to her feet, Marnie stared dumbly at the words on Arthur's T-shirt. BAGSHOT'S MARINE CLEAN, it said. RECYCLE YOUR RUBBISH OR ELSE YOU'RE RUBBISH.

Arthur's eyes widened. 'I saw you underwater! You look just like Christab—'

Marnie spun round and stumbled away as fast as her weird legs could carry her.

'Hey!' Arthur shouted. 'Come back!'

Marnie's heart thumped like a wild thing in her chest. She was in so much trouble. They had to get out of here. Rushing into the crowd, she grabbed Orla with one hand and Eddy with the other. Then she charged towards Pearl and Algie. The next moment, they were all running for the beach as fast as they could.

'Hey!' Arthur shouted behind them.

Marnie scrambled on to the rocks, taking off her human clothing and tossing it behind her. Her friends did the same. They all leaped into the air and splashed into the water, untying Sparkle and diving as deeply and as quickly as they could, swimming away from the shore towards the safety of home.

Despite Orla and Pearl's repeated questions as they swam home through the darkening lagoon, Marnie said nothing about Arthur. As soon as she got home, she rushed into her room and shut the door and curled up under her sea-moss duvet. Arthur was bound to contact Christabel and ask her why Marnie had been at a human music festival. Marnie had a feeling she'd broken about a million mermaid rules, all at once.

Trouble arrived the following morning, as the morning light stole down through the water of the lagoon and filtered through Marnie's seaweed curtains.

'MARNIE!' Christabel shouted.

Marnie swam nervously out of her bedroom. Her aunt was floating in the door of the cave, holding up a seaweed note. There was a dangerous look in her eye.

'Did you go ashore last night, Marnie?' Christabel demanded.

Daphne, Marnie's mum, swam out of her bedroom. 'Did who go ashore?' she asked, yawning.

Christabel swung around. 'Do you know where your daughter was last night, Daffy?'

Marnie's mum rubbed her eyes. 'She went litter-picking with the Brinies, didn't she?'

'Marnie went *ashore*,' said Christabel furiously. 'With hundreds of humans!'

Daphne's mouth dropped open. 'Marnie, is this true?'

Marnie wanted a giant squid to reach its tentacle through the cave window and snatch her up and carry her off. She bit her lip and nodded. Daphne gasped and sat down rather suddenly at the kitchen table.

Christabel waved the seaweed note. 'Can you imagine my surprise, hearing from Arthur this morning that he saw you at a *human music festival*? Of all the reckless things to do! I never thought I'd say it, but this behaviour is too naughty, even for me.'

Marnie squirmed. 'I'm really sorry,' she said. 'I just wanted to find out where the plastic was coming from.'

'And did you?' said Christabel.

'Yes,' said Marnie. 'And I have a plan! Arthur was wearing this thing with words on about recycling, Aunt Christabel. I think he's worried about the plastic too. You could ask him to help—'

'**NO**,' said Christabel. 'Do you want him to get into trouble with Lady Sealia again, like the last time he came to the lagoon?'

Marnie shook her head.

Christabel wagged a finger. 'Do you want her to set sea monsters on him? Because she will!'

Marnie shook her head again, more sadly this time.

'Marnie Blue,' said Daphne, folding her arms. 'You're grounded for—'

A scallop suddenly flapped in through the kitchen window. Christabel snatched it up so quickly that the scallop gave a little squeak of fright.

'Marnie.' Christabel read the note inside the scallop's shell. *'Come to Whale and Hearty! I have a new plan for cleaning up the lagoon and I need your help! From Dora.* Well, **THAT'S** not happening.'

Christabel never got this cross, Marnie thought. It was weird.

'Don't ground me, Mum!' she begged, as Daphne hesitated. 'Dora's plan could be really important for the

78

lagoon. I have to be there.'

'I can't believe you're considering this, Daffy,' said Christabel.

Marnie snatched up her pearl backpack. 'I'll be back as fast as I can,' she said. And she darted out of the cave like an eel.

Chapter Eight

Marnie sped through the drifting plastic, skimming close to the bottom of the lagoon. On the way, she helped to pull a crab's claw out of a McMeaty's cup, and took away a plastic straw that a little fish was nibbling on. 'You'll thank me later,' she told the fish. 'Plastic is NOT good for your tummy.'

Dora's parents ran the Whale and Hearty veterinary surgery. The surgery was a family business. Dora's grandfather had been the first to perform dental surgery on a reef shark. Her grandmother had been the first to perform dental surgery on a reef shark and live to tell the tale. Marnie came to the cluttered, cheerful little surgery with Christabel sometimes, when Garbo needed vitamins or scale polish. It was very close to the bottom of School Rock, so she passed it every day on her way to school.

Marnie swam a little breathlessly into Whale and

Hearty. The others were already there, sitting on a rocky bench underneath posters advertising fish food and sea-worm treatments.

Several other merfolk sat in the surgery too, anxiously holding their pets. There was a catfish with a broken whisker, a pair of tiny striped angelfish tangled sadly together in a loop of plastic netting and a dogfish with a long gash on its side. Marnie wondered if the catfish and dogfish had been injured by plastic as well as the angelfish.

'What happened last night?' said Orla, tickling Sparkle under her golden chin. 'What was the rush?'

'Christabel's ex-boyfriend Arthur was there,' Marnie said. 'He saw me.'

'I knew you should have come back with us,' said Dora, shaking her head.

'Are you in trouble?' Pearl asked.

Marnie nodded. 'He sent Christabel a message. Mum and Christabel were really mad at me and I ALMOST couldn't come but I got away before Mum could ground me.'

'You're getting pretty naughty these days,' said Orla admiringly.

Dora flicked her tail. 'Come on. Everything's outside.'

Marnie followed Pearl, Orla and Dora around the back of the surgery to a small enclosure full of long, thin fish.

'Clingfish!' exclaimed Pearl.

Dora nodded. 'When you pointed out those clingfish yesterday, Pearl, I had an ORCASOME idea,' she said. 'Using clingfish to pick up plastic with their sucker bellies.'

Marnie stared at the squirming clingfish. 'There's hundreds of them,' she said.

'I spent most of last night and this morning collecting and training them,' said Dora proudly. 'They're really clever. You just point at the plastic and they pick it up and drop it into a net and then you give them THIS as a treat.'

She produced a pale lilac blob of something in her hand.

'Is that . . .' said Marnie.

'That's not . . .' said Orla.

'Dolphin poo,' said Dora happily. 'I made loads more. The clingfish can't get enough of it.'

Marnie pictured the lagoon with all the McMeaty's cartons and bottles picked up by the clingfish. 'This is your best clean-up idea EVER,' she gasped. 'You'll DEFINITELY get your Brinies Inventor badge now!'

Dora handed out bags of dolphin-poo treats to

Marnie, Pearl and Orla. The clingfish twisted and squirmed eagerly. 'Just be firm,' she said. 'They can be a bit nervous.'

The clingfish swarmed around the mermaids in a big brown cloud. Sparkle swam in and out of Pearl's hair, steering clear of the clingfish's sticky bellies.

'NO, you naughty fish,' Orla said, peeling a clingfish off her tail and trying to hide her dolphin-poo treats. 'We haven't started work yet.'

The four mermaids swam to the bottom of School Rock, where the plastic debris lay in heaps and drifts. The clingfish followed them as they set up their net.

'FETCH!' said Marnie.

She pointed at a plastic bottle. A clingfish shot away and suckered on to the bottle at once. Before Marnie had even asked, it swam to the net and dropped the plastic. It was back at Marnie's side in moments, snuffling eagerly at the treat in her hand.

'Whoo!' said Orla as four clingfish zoomed around her with boxes and straws stuck to their bellies. 'This is so COOL!'

Marnie could barely see Pearl or Orla through the cloud of clingfish darting left and right and up and down. The net was filling up.

'This is brilliant!' said Pearl. 'It already feels like there's hardly any plastic left. We'll clean everything up in one go!'

Something long and shadowy swam slowly into view.

The clingfish stopped dead, hovering in the water. Sensing danger.

Before Marnie had time to shout, 'SHARK!' — because it was, indeed, a shark — hundreds of nervous clingfish rocketed up School Rock, with hundreds of plastic bottles and boxes and straws and lids stuck to their tummies, heading for the biggest, safest cave that they could see. Then hundreds of clingfish and hundreds of bits of plastic vanished from view.

'Whoops,' said Dora.

'Ah,' said Orla.

'Where did they go?' said Pearl.

Marnie gazed up at School Rock. 'I think they all went into the Assembly Cave.'

'DOUBLE whoops,' said Dora.

Orla whistled.

'After all that effort the teachers went to, to keep the plastic out of school this week!' gasped Pearl.

'At least the sea bed is clean now,' Orla said.

Heavy with bottles and boxes, the mermaids' net swayed on its coral branches. There wasn't a scrap of plastic left on the rocky ground around School Rock.

Marnie tried to gather her thoughts. 'I'm going up there to see,' she said. 'It might not be so bad.'

'Watch out for Lady Sealia,' said Dora.

'It's the weekend,' said Orla. 'She won't be there.'

'Better safe than sorry,' Pearl said. 'She will TURTLY expel us.'

Marnie swam cautiously up the face of School Rock to the mouth of the Assembly Cave. Hundreds of clingfish swam out as she approached, and scattered like little brown sea snakes in hundreds of different directions. There was no plastic on their bellies any more. Which meant . . .

Marnie's heart sank into her tail.

Hundreds of pieces of McMeaty's plastic were piled up inside the Assembly Cave. They swayed and tottered in piles and drifts. The stage was completely covered. The coral stools were buried underneath the bottles, boxes and straws.

Marnie wanted to curl up into a tiny sea-snail shell and die.

'It's bad,' said Orla behind her.

'Really bad,' Marnie groaned.

'Bad enough for Lady Sealia to expel us?' said Pearl, swimming in with Dora and looking at the mess with wide eyes.

'Maybe we can clear it up before anyone notices,' Marnie said.

They all gazed at the mountains of junk hiding the portraits of Lady Sealia that hung on the walls.

'Right,' said Orla. 'And Miss Tinkle has thirteen tentacles.'

They swam silently back to the Whale and Hearty surgery. Marnie tried to stay positive. If they could empty the cave before Lady Sealia got back, no one would be expelled. They just had to make a PLAN.

And ideally figure something out before her mum got mad that she wasn't back yet, and grounded her forever.

Thinking about Daphne made Marnie feel worried. This was all taking much longer than she had expected.

They arrived at the surgery at the same time as a wild-eyed mermaid with a long pink sea-moss coat, sparkly sunglasses and a huge pair of crystal earrings.

'Aunt Christabel?' said Marnie. With a horrible lurch in her stomach, she saw Garbo, lying motionless in her aunt's hands.

There was a quiver in the voice of the most famous mermaid in the lagoon.

'Garbo ate some sparkly plastic,' Christabel said tearfully. 'And I'm scared that she's going to die!'

Chapter Nine

Marnie, Pearl, Orla and Dora waited anxiously in the little reception area of Whale and Hearty. Dora's mum had swum into action straight away, taking the little goldfish into the small operating theatre at the back of the cave. Christabel had gone with her.

It felt like the longest wait in the world.

Marnie jumped off the coral bench when Christabel came slowly out of the operating theatre.

'Is Garbo OK?' said Pearl. She was cuddling Sparkle very tightly.

'I don't know yet,' said Christabel. She sank on to the bench. 'I have to wait.'

Marnie squeezed her aunt's hand. 'I'm sure Garbo is going to be all right, Aunt Christabel,' she said, even though she wasn't sure at all. 'Dora's mum is a brilliant vet.'

Christabel sniffed. 'Look at me,' she said, wiping her eyes. 'My make-up is a wreck. This plastic pollution has to stop!'

The starfish clock on the wall scratched itself. It was moving very slowly. To take her aunt's mind off Garbo, Marnie told Christabel about the clingfish dumping all the plastic in the Assembly Cave, and how furious Lady Sealia would be, and how they didn't know when she would be coming back into school, or how to stop her from finding out what had happened.

'We didn't do it on purpose,' Marnie said. 'But she won't believe us. She never does.'

'We're SO expelled,' said Pearl gloomily.

Christabel put her face in her hands. Her shoulders shook.

'Please don't cry,' said Marnie anxiously. 'Aunt Christabel?'

Christabel sat up and wiped her eyes for a second

time. 'I'm not crying,' she said. 'Oh, Marnie! That's cheered me right up. What is it about the Blue family that makes us such disasters? It's not so bad, you know. The sea bed is clean, and the junk is all in one place. Even if that place is Mermaid School.'

'We need to get it out of there before Lady Sealia comes back,' said Marnie. 'Aunt Christabel, I really think Arthur could help. He knows about recycling. His shirt said so. "Bagshot's Marine Clean", it said. I wanted to ask him about clearing up the plastic AND taking it away – but now we've got it all inside Mermaid School, he can just do the taking away bit.'

Christabel sighed. 'I could ask, I suppose,' she said. Marnie crossed her fingers and her fins. 'Will you? Please?'

Christabel glanced at the door of the operating theatre. Then she looked back at Marnie. 'Yes,' she said with a nod. 'I will.'

Marnie threw her arms around her aunt. 'If Arthur can take away all the plastic before Lady Sealia comes into school, she never has to find out that we were the ones that put it there!'

'We're so **NOT** expelled!' said Pearl happily. She kissed Sparkle's nose.

Christabel held up her hand. 'Arthur won't get the message today. He could come tomorrow? With his boat, of course.'

'But that's too late,' said Marnie. 'Lady Sealia is bound to come into school later. She's always around. We have to fix this today, Aunt Christabel!'

'We're **SO** expelled, all over again,' said Pearl, gloomy again.

'What about the dolphin?' said Orla suddenly.

'What dolphin?' asked Christabel.

'Yes!' Marnie gasped. 'The dolphin can take the message for us!'

'You know a dolphin?' said Christabel.

'She promised that she would come if we needed her,' said Pearl, clapping her hands. 'And dolphins are mega-fast. Arthur could be here in a couple of hours!'

'WHAT DOLPHIN?' said Christabel.

Marnie quickly explained about the net and the dolphin's promise.

'You are the most surprising niece I've ever had,' Christabel said in astonishment.

Marnie and her friends swam out of the surgery, calling and shouting and waving their arms. 'Help! Help! Please, lovely special dolphin, help us!'

All the fish outside the surgery scattered. Excited by the noise, Sparkle did five loops in a row. But there was no sign of a dolphin.

'Wait,' said Marnie. 'We have to call her by her name. Her name was all those whistles and clicks . . .'

They whistled and clicked a few times. The name was soft, loud, soft, loud — Marnie remembered that much. *Click-PEEP-peep-CLICK* . . . or something. *Peep-PEEP-peep-CLICK-PEEP* . . . They tried them all in different combinations. Still nothing happened.

'Imagine if we're saying lots of really rude things in dolphin language,' said Pearl. 'What was that rhythm thing you did with the name, Orla?'

Orla snapped her fingers. 'Of course! It was *Gil-ly SEA-FLO-WER is a BLOB-FISH.*'

'Not BLOB-FISH,' said Marnie. 'TWIT.'

94

Orla screwed her face up tightly and puffed out her cheeks. *'Peep peep CLICK CLICK-CLICK click click PEEEEP!'* she said.

And there — magically and suddenly — was the dolphin, pale grey and smiling in the warm lagoon water in front of them. Marnie could still see the marks where the net had injured her skin.

'Krilliant, Orla!' gasped Dora.

'Neptune's knickers,' said Christabel, watching from the door of the surgery. 'You really do know a dolphin.'

'And one who is happy to help,' said the dolphin.

'Can you take a message for us, please?' asked Marnie. She pulled open her backpack and took out some seaweed paper and a shell pen.

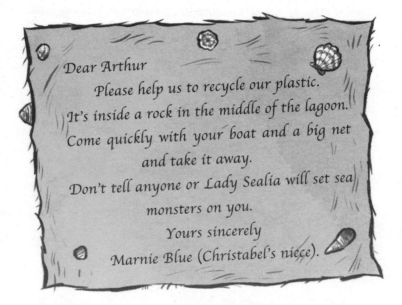

Dear Arthur
    Please help us to recycle our plastic.
It's inside a rock in the middle of the lagoon.
Come quickly with your boat and a big net
        and take it away.
Don't tell anyone or Lady Sealia will set sea
        monsters on you.
        Yours sincerely
    Marnie Blue (Christabel's niece).

'It's for a human called Arthur,' Marnie said as she folded up the seaweed note. 'Can you find him?'

The dolphin put her head on one side. 'Don't you know where he is?'

'He's probably on his boat,' said Marnie.

'There are many boats around the lagoon,' said the dolphin. 'How will I know which one is his?'

96

'It's called the *Christabel*,' said Christabel. She blushed. 'He named it after me.'

'So romantic,' Pearl sighed.

Marnie carefully tucked the message into the dolphin's beak. 'Look for a boat with the name *Christabel* on it,' she said. 'This means everything, to us, and to our lagoon. Be as quick as you can. Thank you!'

The dolphin flicked her tail and was gone, as quickly as she had appeared.

'Ms Blue?'

Christabel spun round at the sound of Dr Agua's voice. 'Is Garbo—'

Dr Agua's wide, friendly face split into a warm smile. 'Garbo is fine. You can take her home now.'

Christabel threw her arms around Dora's mother.

'I'll dedicate the whole of my next *Big Blue Show* to you and Whale and Hearty, Dr Agua,' she said in delight. 'You're an absolute marvel.'

'I told you it would be OK,' said Marnie, putting her arm around her aunt's waist. She smiled, imagining the dolphin swimming swiftly towards Arthur. '*Everything* is going to be OK.'

The Last
Chapter

Christabel took Garbo home while Marnie and Pearl waited at the Whale and Hearty surgery. Orla was posted a short distance from School Rock, to check that Lady Sealia wasn't on her way into school. Every now and again, Marnie, Dora and Pearl swam up to the surface of the lagoon to look for an approaching boat. Dora and Pearl brought up the net that the clingfish had filled as well, and dumped it with the rest.

'How long do you think we've got?' Pearl said as they studied the horizon. 'Before Lady Sealia turns up?'

'She might not come into school at all,' said Dora.

But no one could say for sure.

'It's good there's no roof,' said Marnie. The Assembly Cave was right at the top of School Rock and opened straight out onto the surface of the lagoon. 'I'm counting on that when Arthur comes. We've cleared up all the plastic on the sea bed, so he only needs to take it away now. He can lower his net into the cave, and we can put all the plastic inside.' She bit her nails. 'Oh, where is he?'

She suddenly heard a droning sound. An engine, coming from the east. She gripped Pearl's arm. Was that Arthur's boat?

'Ow,' protested Pearl. Sparkle growled.

Marnie apologised and let go. The droning was getting louder. The top of the lagoon started rippling with waves.

Dora looked as white as a moonfish. 'Gilly says humans eat mermaids,' she said. 'They eat them and spit out their bones.'

Dora didn't know anything about humans at all. Marnie felt very grown-up in comparison. 'Jellyfish gibberish,' she said firmly. 'Arthur won't eat us.'

The boat came into view. Marnie could read the name painted on its prow: *Christabel*. Dora gave a frightened squeal and disappeared beneath the water.

'I'll go check on Orla,' Pearl said. She ducked under the surface as well, leaving Marnie by herself.

Marnie sank down into the lagoon so that only her eyes were showing. She could see Arthur at the prow of the boat. And at the back . . . Marnie's heart jumped into her mouth. There was another human on the deck of the *Christabel*!

Arthur's head popped over the boat rail. He was wearing his funny diving suit again, with his mask on the top of his head. He smiled down at Marnie in the water and put his finger to his lips. *Stay quiet.*

'What are we doing here, boss?' said the second human.

'I told you, Troy,' Arthur said. 'I got a tip-off about a load of plastic washing up inside this bit of rock. I'll dive down and fill the big net. You're here to winch it up.'

'Who gave you the tip-off?' Troy sounded suspicious. 'No one ever comes this far into the lagoon.'

'Have you got the net or not?' said Arthur.

Grumbling, Troy went into the cabin. Arthur leaned over the boat rail again. 'Troy wouldn't believe me if I told him the tip-off came from a dolphin,' he said quietly to Marnie.

Marnie looked up at Arthur's kind blue eyes. 'Can you take the plastic away and recycle it?'

Arthur nodded. 'We've already cleared the beach where the festival took place. We found seaweed nets full of plastic parcelled up neatly on the rocks,' he added, looking curiously at Marnie. 'Was that anything to do with you?'

Marnie grinned and nodded. She was pleased Arthur had found it all. 'Will the music festival come back and fill our lagoon with plastic again?'

'No,' said Arthur firmly. 'I complained to the festival organiser about the mess and the damage to the lagoon wildlife. Today was the last day, thank goodness. Next year, no one's going to litter the lagoon with junk.'

Marnie couldn't resist a little somersault of joy. Arthur laughed.

'What are you laughing at?' Troy shouted from the back of the boat.

'Nothing!' Arthur called. 'See you down there,' he whispered to Marnie, and he put on his diving mask.

Marnie ducked back under the water. She saw Pearl swimming up towards her.

'Lady Sealia and Dilys are coming!' Pearl said urgently. 'Orla's doing her best to delay them, but time is running out.'

Marnie felt a rush of fear. If Lady Sealia saw Arthur with his diving suit and his boat, she would freak out. There'd be SERIOUS consequences — and not just for Arthur.

She heard a splash above her. Arthur had dropped into the lagoon and was guiding the big net as it was lowered through the gap in the Assembly Cave roof. Dora turned a funny green colour at the sight of Arthur's diving suit.

'Don't be scared, Dora,' said Marnie. 'He's *helping* us. Come on!'

They swam around, scooping armfuls of bottles and straws into the net as it settled on the cave floor. Dora stayed as far away from Arthur as she could. Arthur himself swam about clumsily, staring around at the Assembly Cave in wonder. Marnie had to untangle the net from the coral stools they all sat on during assembly. One of Lady Sealia's portraits fell off the wall and almost dropped into the net as well.

'Whoops,' Pearl panted, struggling to hang the portrait back on the wall. 'Get out of the net, Sparkle!'

They had put most of the plastic into the net when Marnie heard voices outside the Cave. She and the others froze.

'. . . the biggest reef shark you ever saw, Lady Sealia. You don't want to go in there.'

'I've lived in this lagoon for many years, Orla.' Lady Sealia sounded testy. 'The reef sharks are more scared of ME than I am of THEM.'

'But it's got, like, a million teeth!' Orla went on. 'Honestly, it's super-massive. And I heard its tummy rumbling. It's going to eat you if you go inside.'

'Out of my way now. I have work to do, and Dilys needs her din-dins.'

Arthur's eyes were wide behind his mask. Marnie exchanged frantic looks with Dora and Pearl. Orla had to keep Lady Sealia outside the cave!

'But what if Dilys gets eaten, Lady Sealia?' Orla said.

Marnie threw another armful of cartons into the net. Dora, Pearl and Arthur did the same.

'Dilys?' said Lady Sealia. 'You think it might eat Dilys?'

'Oh, definitely! It's bigger than the biggest shark in the whole entire world and I'm not even joking, cross my fins and hope to die,' Orla rattled on. 'AND I saw the tail of a dogfish in its mouth when it swam inside the Assembly Cave and I thought maybe it had eaten Dilys ALREADY.'

Marnie and Arthur shoved more straws, boxes and lids into the net. Pearl rescued Sparkle for a second time. There was just one bottle left in the corner of the cave. Dora lobbed it into the net like a professional fishball player.

'I wish to see this wicked dogfish-eating shark for myself!' said Lady Sealia.

Arthur tugged twice on the net as soon as it was full. He nodded at Marnie, saluted Pearl and Dora (Dora giggled) and swam up to the surface. Marnie heard the thrum of boat machinery overhead. The net began to move, swaying as it was winched up towards the surface.

She felt something tug at her. To her horror, her tail was caught in the net.

'Come, Dilys,' Lady Sealia said outside the cave.

'We shall see this nasty shark for ourselves— what in Neptune's name is that noise?'

'It's the mega-enormous shark BREATHING,' Orla said shrilly. 'I told you it was big!''

Dangling upside down, Marnie desperately tried to untangle herself. The thrum of machinery was louder than ever as it pulled the net towards the surface. Marnie wriggled and pulled. It was no good. She was stuck.

'Marnie!' cried Pearl and Dora in horror.

'MOVE ASIDE!' commanded Lady Sealia.

And that was the last Marnie heard as she was winched above the surface of the lagoon.

This Turtley is **The Last Chapter**

Marnie wriggled and yanked desperately to free her tail. Her hair trailed in the water as she dangled upside down. This was it. This was the end. The other human would see her and take her away and eat her, just like Dora and Gilly had said.

Arthur appeared at the prow of the boat with his diving mask on the top of his head. Marnie looked helplessly at his upside-down face.

'Better get this lot on board,' she heard Troy say. 'I'll come round to the front and help you pull—'

'NO!' said Arthur. He stretched towards Marnie but his fingers didn't quite reach. 'I can do it myself . . .'

'Don't be daft.' Marnie could hear Troy clomping along the deck towards the prow. 'This is a two-man job. I'll—'

SPLASH! Arthur leaped off the boat and paddled

towards Marnie. 'I'll get you out,' he whispered. 'Stay still.'

'Man overboard!' cried Troy in horror.

There was a knife in Arthur's hand now. He made a little cut in the net. Marnie's tail slithered free.

'**WHOA!** Big fish!' she heard Troy shout as she

plopped into the water like a stone.

She had landed outside School Rock. With a hammering heart, she paddled down as quickly as she could to the Assembly Cave entrance. Smoothing her ruffled scales and trying to stay calm, she swam inside.

'I just saw this MEGA shark jumping out of the Assembly Cave,' she announced a little breathlessly. 'It was honestly the size of a whale.'

Lady Sealia swung around, clutching Dilys. Orla and Dora clapped their hands across their mouths. Sparkle squeaked as Pearl squeezed her too hard.

'It was completely huge,' Marnie continued. 'I'm surprised you didn't see it.'

Orla sat down on one of the coral stools. 'I told you, Lady Sealia,' she said. 'I told you it was a shark.'

'I . . .' said Lady Sealia.

'It **JUMPED** out through the top of the Assembly Cave roof like a dolphin,' said Marnie. She was getting into her story now. 'It had some kind of breathing problem because it was snorting **REALLY** loudly. Like a . . . human boat, or something.'

'A human boat,' Lady Sealia repeated.

'I can hear the **MASSIVE SHARK** swimming away now,' Dora piped up.

They all listened to the chugging of Arthur's boat as it faded into the distance.

'Where did all the plastic go?' said Lady Sealia at last.

There was a horrible pause.

'What plastic?' said Orla feebly.

'The plastic which has been spoiling the lagoon all week,' Lady Sealia said. 'The plastic which prevented your PE lesson. The plastic that you were all protesting about during the Fishball Final and cleaning up on your Brinies expedition last night. It was out there.' She waved out of the Assembly Cave. 'And now it's . . . not.'

'Maybe the shark took it,' said Pearl brightly. 'I heard that humans train sharks these days, to clean up the oceans.'

'My brain does not have tail rot, Pearl,' said Lady Sealia. 'What *really* happened?'

'I trained lots of clingfish to pick up the plastic, Lady Sealia,' said Dora, with a touch of pride. 'With dolphin poo.' She held out a dolphin-poo treat as proof. 'And then . . . the shark took it. Like Pearl said.'

Lady Sealia wrinkled her nose at the mention of dolphin poo. 'If the clingfish part is true, that is commendable, Dora,' she said at last. 'And I have to say, it is very pleasant to have an uninterrupted view of the lagoon again. Perhaps . . . we will let the matter drop. For now.'

'You need a nice hot cup of kelp tea, Lady Sealia,' said Orla soothingly.

'Yes. Kelp tea,' Lady Sealia murmured. Her eyes grew distant. 'And perhaps a biscuit.'

Marnie grinned with relief at her friends. They grinned back. Mission accomplished.

'Din-dins, Dilys,' the headteacher of Mermaid School said at last, looking at her pet dogfish. 'Come!'

What is Your Mermaid Name?

Find the month of your birthday and your favourite colour to reveal your o*fish*al mermaid identity!

January	Coral
February	Delta
March	Shelly
April	Hallie
May	Nerissa
June	Andrina
July	Harmony
August	Lorelei
September	Marina
October	Serena
November	Cordelia
December	Melinda

Blue	Seagrass
Green	Kelp
Purple	Triton
Gold	Shore
White	Smallcove
Red	Fairweather
Pink	Waverly
Black	Tidesmith
Yellow	Fishmonger
Turquoise	Waters
Orange	Mangrove
Silver	Sandragon

MERMAID SCHOOL

LUCY COURTENAY
ILLUSTRATED BY SHEENA DEMPSEY

Collect them all!